HARMONY

The Legend of Forest Ranch

Harmony: The Legend of Forest Ranch
Copyright © 2022 by Wilma Forester

Published in the United States of America

ISBN   Paperback: 978-1-959165-72-9
ISBN   Hardback: 978-1-959165-91-0
ISBN   eBook: 978-1-959165-73-6

All rights reserved. No part of this publication may be reproduced, stored in a retrieval system or transmitted in any way by any means, electronic, mechanical, photocopy, recording or otherwise without the prior permission of the author except as provided by USA copyright law.

The opinions expressed by the author are not necessarily those of ReadersMagnet, LLC.

ReadersMagnet, LLC
10620 Treena Street, Suite 230 | San Diego, California, 92131 USA
1.619. 354. 2643 | www.readersmagnet.com

Book design copyright © 2022 by ReadersMagnet, LLC. All rights reserved.

Cover design by Ericka Obando
Interior design by Daniel Lopez

Harmony

The Legend of Forest Ranch

Wilma Forester

ReadersMagnet, LLC

Oh hurry, come over here and look at that still wet rock, you can see tiny circles of gold dust like a miniature horse's hoof prints, what magic could this be? Look close! Perhaps a Harmony is near. O.K. so what is a Harmony? It is a tiny playful horse-like creature that looks like it's made of glass. It has a white fuzzy mane and tail, two sparkling bright eyes and wings like a dragonfly. Since they are only about four inches tall, they may easily sit in the palm of your hand. Shining in the sunlight they can quickly dart from a rock to the sky and dance back to earth again, almost before you can blink your eye. Listen, did you hear a soft haunting melody or is it just the water bubbling over the rocks?

I would like to tell you a fascinating story about an Indian Legend that has been told and retold from parent to child for many generations. An old man in the little town of Forest Ranch told me because it happened very close to the town he called it the "Legend of Forest Ranch".

My husband Gene, our two children plus myself had just moved to this small town which is nestled in a mostly evergreen forest in the mountains of northern California; the population was about 1,000 at this time in 1965 or thereabout. We were pleasantly surrounded with Cedar, Pine, Oak, Sugar pine, and many other trees, like the beautiful Dogwood trees which bloom with the white flowers in the spring. I was very excited to be living in such a pretty little town and everything and everybody were so nice to us. I wanted to explore and enjoy it all!

One day I was walking with my children Jeff and Brenda (Rolls). We meandered close to the one room schoolhouse, which sits off the main road near a little stream (which only runs when it rains). Then we strolled under some very tall pine trees. It was a beautiful fall morning, with the air feeling so fresh and cool. Even a bit of frost was left in the tree shadows along the trail. As we walked on up the lane, I felt so happy that we weren't in a hurry this morning. Soon we passed near this big old snarled tree with a weathered sign nailed on it; the - **World's Largest Cherry tree** - it read.

The roots of it twisted beneath a rectangular shaped cement watering trough, with the words "Diamond Match Co.," imprinted into the side. There was a cold, clean spring of water flowing over the cracked side of the trough and it smoothly collected into several nice puddles in the middle of the road, (all of this plus some pretty colored rocks). We stopped to admire this lovely bit of history and the children immediately began to stick their fingers into the trickling water to touch the shiny pebbles. They were having such fun! Even the plain looking dry rocks on the road nearby became sparkling shades of green, gray, coral and gold when they were dipped into the water.

It was then I noticed the elderly gentleman propped against the fence post, catching the morning sunlight on his weathered, frowning face. He wore red suspenders over a denim shirt with patches on the elbows and it seemed to fit so perfectly with him and this new little town we were in. He even had a long white beard. It was like the picture you might expect to see of old father time only he was a little thinner and more worn looking. I turned and looked at him and spoke first, "If this old tree could talk I bet it could tell many stories." He slowly nodded his head up and down. "Well this old tree can't talk but I can," he replied. We later became good friends and it was true he could talk and talk, and TALK!! He called it a spinning yarn.

We later spent many enjoyable hours doing just that and one of the stories that I heard from him was the "Harmony Legend of Forest Ranch." So if you please, I would like to retell that story to you, so now it is my TURN to spin a yarn...

The Elderly Gentleman

CHAPTER ONE

So here goes my story: Once upon a time many years ago near what is now called the town of Forest Ranch; there lived a large tribe of Indians. Their settlement was very close to what the local people call the Forks of the Butte. They lived in the nearby meadows.

The Indian Chief was a wise good leader named Tyanne (which means wise one). Tyanne had a beautiful daughter named Melody, and a son named Dragon-fly, and they were twins. They must have been mirror or reverse twins because Dragon-fly was just as evil as Melody was kind, and gentle. They could not agree on anything.

Melody and Dragonfly

Wait a minute this story is about the Legendary Harmonies that I talked about on page one of this book. Well don't worry I will tell you more about them. You see Harmonies were originally created to send out feelings of happiness and good will to everyone, even other animal creatures, but it wasn't working. Because of the terrible battles and bad feeling between the White men and the Indians, all Harmonies were ordered to leave the West. Only two were left and they were grieving and sad. Dusty and Silky were two Harmonies that had been ordered to stay behind. They were hiding out by the big water fall called the Heart Shaped Pool. Old Master Tory Toad was in charge of all Harmony hatchings and happening, and he had declared there would be NO more young Harmonies until things greatly improved in the West.

Then one beautiful summer day, "Oh, who are you?", asked a young Indian girl. It was Melody she had gone to sing her songs by the waterfall. Because she had been crying, Dusty had disobeyed the rules as he often did, and he flew right down near her. At first she was a bit startled to see this mysterious creature jumping and flitting in and out of the wildflowers. But soon Silky, the bossier one of the two, flew after Dusty and scolded him. He sooo wanted to give good feelings and happiness to this sad girl. When Silky saw Melody's falling tears she too forgot all about the rules and fluttered down to join him. Soon Melody was not frightened or crying. She was laughing and holding out her hands to the two playful, flying Harmonies. After that day she came to see them whenever she was lonely or sad. The three became very good friends but she never told anyone about them.

Sometime later in my YARN, a very nice young man from the East came searching for gold. His name was Harlan. The life of a

Gold miner was very difficult in those days (still is today) but he had traveled many, many miles to come here and so he was willing to work very hard.

What you need to know is, finding the Gold was only the first step, getting it in the pan took time and skill and a strong back. Harlan being raised and educated in the East knew very little about Gold mining. He had to learn a lot of things the hard way but then he began to watch the other miners as they worked and soon he was doing O.K. He built a sluice box first to shovel the rich gravel through and then he panned the tailings out by hand. He would sit close to the stream's edge and swirl the fine dark sand around and around in a large metal pan. (Gold pan) He was often rewarded with bright yellow nuggets shining through the black sand. It was quiet and pleasant working by himself and listening to the sounds of the stream and watching the birds and other creature's nearby. He loved the serene beauty of the evergreen forest and he made many friends in the little town of Forest Ranch.

Harlan panned for Gold

Then one day he was quite surprised to hear music, very pleasant singing coming from somewhere up on the mountains. He put down the Gold pan and climbed up toward the meadow and listened. You guessed it! It was Melody. A few days later she passed by again and he caught sight of her riding her spotted pony. He was enchanted and managed to see her again and again. What happened? Just to keep a long story short (maybe it's is already too late) I'll tell you in one line. He fell in love with her and promised her that he will build her a home in the nearby meadows and they would be married.

The Favorite Meeting Place

They spent many wonderful hours riding their horses together. They shared stories of their childhood and what their life at home was like and dreamed of what their life together might become someday. The Heart Shaped pool near the waterfall was a favorite meeting place for them.

This large beautiful pool is still there today; it is along Big Chico creek. It is surrounded by steep rocky canyon walls (high up over head) and has a big waterfall just above it which splashes down the rocks and into the pool. Today it is called "Bear Lake." It is very close to Forest Ranch but there are no roads leading to it and the trail is long and rough. You can find it on most geological maps of this area.

CHAPTER TWO

The story takes a very wrong turn... Dragon-fly (her brother) was in a very different frame of mind; he hated the miners, because they mudded the streams and ruined the good hunting and fishing. He especially hated Harlan because not only was he a Gold miner but he spent so much time with his sister Melody. He was jealous and angry and often complained to his father Tyanne but to no avail. However, the rest of the Indian tribe was prospering because of the trade of animal furs and also many new jobs were available working in the Gold mines. No one else was unhappy about the loggers and miners being there, just Dragonfly.

One day in secret he made a visit to the Witch Doctor, who was known for his power of making evil spells and curses. Together they made some very wicked plans. Meanwhile back at the stream, "Glory Hole", that's what it was. Harlan found a cache of gold in the bottom of the Heart shaped pool. However, what he never knew was how this cache of gold came to be there for him to find. You see someone had worked very hard during the night before and uncovered all that gold. It was Dusty and Silky!

"Come on Silky, catch up with me, we must help Harlan find the gold," it was Dusty. For quite some time now, the two of them had secretly been watching the budding romance of Harlan and Melody.

They noticed how happy and smiling Melody had become and they wanted to hurry things up and help Harlan find the illusive load of gold that he was searching so hard for. Now Harmonies know a lot about gold. Yes, remember I told you about the tiny golden hoof prints they leave where ever they walk along the ground.

"Oh no Dusty we can't interfere in the affairs' of humans, not with Out Master Tory Toads' approval!" said Silky. She was always so careful, thought Dusty.

"But Silky, we must do it tonight when no one is around to see us. Come quick: and follow me!" he said. And she did. It was getting dark but Harmonies see quite well in the dark. First by sniffing with their noses, they found a pocket of nice nuggets; above the waterfall and by working very hard; they dug until they uncovered it. Then they 'laid a trail of golden hoof prints for Harlan to see when he came to work in the morning. But as they were cleaning up and moving some gravel in the stream below the waterfall, Dusty got his front foot caught in a pile of rocks.

"Oh OUCH I am stuck, help help!" he whispered. Harmonies have very soft bell like voices, but Silky heard him and she came as fast as she could fly.

"I told you we should not be doing this, now look what has happened. You may be stuck here until morning, and then every one will find you not them? You know we would be in BAD trouble," she whispered. He was twisting and flopping around while getting his beautiful wings; all muddy. *"Now will you please quit jumping around and I will get you out!"* After looking the situation over, first Silky quickly dug a hole with her front feet, she looked like a dog digging for a bone, and then she turned and pushed like a mad mule with her back hoofs. After several tries Dusty popped free and floated downstream a bit.

He soon caught hold of a small boulder and carefully washed the mud off his delicate wings. Remember Harmonies hate dirt! Then off they went flying, along together.

But, *"Oh dear,"* thought Silky, *"Dusty is flying a little crocked. What is wrong with him?"*

Meanwhile when morning came, "glory hole, Harlan shouted!" He was so excited, there was enough gold for all his and Melody's plans and dreams. Also in this nice pocket of gold there was a beautiful large nugget with a shiny, clear quartz crystal stuck through it. He put them both in his pocket. Later he fashioned it into a necklace for Melody. He showed her how the two pieces fit together perfectly. Harlan asked her to always wear this special crystal necklace as a token reminder of his love for her. He wore the matching piece of the gold nugget.

They both realized that he needed to return home and inform his parents of all the wonderful things that had happened and then get his personal things and make plans for their life together. Melody designed a beautiful deerskin bag and decorated it with crystal quarts' beads and white stones. The pattern on the front of the pouch was two tiny shining white horses with wings. (Who do you think she was remembering?) She lovingly gave the bag to Harlan to use on his trip homeward. She promised to wear the crystal necklace he had made for her and to wait for his return.

"I'll be back next spring when the first Dogwood flowers are in bloom!" he promised her. They rode through the meadow once more to say goodbye, vowing to love and wait for one another forever. They were so much in love it was plain for all to see!

Harlan put the largest of the nuggets in the special deerskin bag, and left on his horse for the city of Chico. With a good horse you could easily make Chico in one day, and Harlan had a good horse. His name was Stick. He got the strange name because his mane would not lay down the way it should. It would just stick up so they just called him "Stick" When he arrived he found a safe place to board Stick and leave the mining tools and all his personal things. Then catching the Stage coach, he began his long trip home to the East, where he lived with his parents. He would return in the spring with the plans and material for their dream cabin in the meadows. He swore that when the dogwood (the beautiful white flowers that grow all around Forest Ranch) began to bloom in the spring Melody could look for his return.

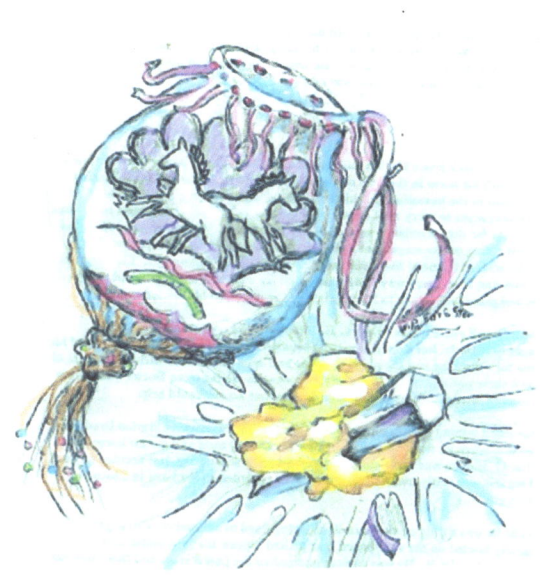

But many years passed and Harlan did not return! Melody watched and waited but when she saw the Dogwood flowers bloom every spring, her heart grew sad and her songs ceased. She often sat alone by the Heart Shaped Pool and thought about him and now much she loved him. She had truly trusted him, to keep his word.

Dusty and Silky tried to cheer her up but no one could make her smile again. Then one day in bitter disappointment and anger she threw the crystal necklace, which he had made for her, into the pool. The next day she was sorry and she jumped into the water and tried to retrieve it but the water was too deep and cold and no matter how hard she tried the crystal necklace couldn't be found. In the following days she became very quiet and withdrawn and even quit riding her spotted pony. Chief Tyanne, her father, was very worried about her and thought she must be ill. So he sent her to live in another village with his many friends where perhaps she might forget all about Harlan and recover.

Her brother Dragon-fly often taunted her, *"Don't wait for that evil lying white man because he will never return!"* The truth was, in secret he and the Witch Doctor had met and put an evil CURSE on the Heart Shaped Pool and Harlan. The spell of this CURSE could only be broken if all the gold that was taken from the pool was returned into it.

Harlan left his horse at the barn

CHAPTER THREE

....

Can we step back in time a little bit here? Remember when Harlan first started his trip back to his home in the East? Let's look at what happened that first day. It was a long ride to Chico. He rode first to the old barn on the edge of town. There he left his horse in the care of a friend. Very early that next morning when no one else was around, Harlan carefully hid the beautiful deerskin bag full of gold nuggets beneath a loose board in the barn floor. He felt it was too dangerous to carry all of it with him and besides he would need some money to pay for the lumber and other building material on his return to Chico. He thought no one had seen him hide it. But he was wrong. Later after he said goodbye to Stick he stepped aboard the Stagecoach and departed.

His joy of returning home was short lived. His parents were angry and disappointed that he wanted to spend his life in the West and with an Indian girl. They· just didn't understand why he wanted to do such a thing. They argued with him and tried every way to discourage it, but Harlan was very determined to continue working out he plans and return to Melody before the white flowers bloomed, just the way he had promised her.

But very soon the evil CURSE began to work. Harlan often held the gold nugget necklace in his hand and thought of Melody, but slowly, very slowly he became confused and soon he lost all memory of his reason for wanting to return. He even forgot his promises' and all the plans they had made. His beloved Melody was fading from mind. All of this was happening because of the EVIL CURSE put on him by Dragonfly and the Witch Doctor. He went to see the town Physician because he felt so ill. He knew something was very wrong with him but no one could help him. He began to wander about the country aimlessly, he was not himself!

Then one day Harlan received a surprise visitor. It was a mining friend all the way from Forest Ranch. This man had worked with him in his gold mining adventures. He had come from the West to the town where Harlan was living and asked him when he was going to return for his mining tools and get his horse at the old barn? Harlan was astonished and said the man was mixed-up; there must be some mistake. Finally, he agreed to go and see if it was really true. They made the return trip back to Chico, California together. First: of all he went to the old barn to investigate. It WAS true! His tools and his horse, Stick, were still there! *"What was happening to him?"*

Harlan sat down on the barn floor in a daze trying to remember everything. Then a strange thing happened. There came an odd looking whitish dragonfly or butterfly. It landed on a loose board on the barn floor and disappeared underneath it. *"Hmmm, what was that thing? I think maybe, it was Silky?"* He was so curious he pulled the board up and there to his astonishment was the deerskin bag Melody had made for him. The bag with the two shinning white horses and it was still full of all the gold nuggets. Slowly, slowly he began to remember bits and pieces of all the past events. Melody, oh Melody, would she still be there? would she still love me?" he wondered. He immediately saddled his horse and rode up to Forest Ranch. He went first to the Heart Shaped Pool, hoping Melody might be there, but she was not to be found. As he rode along he prayed to God, please let me find her so we can be together again!

Chief Tyanne quickly heard of his return and rode to meet him. He told Harlan about all the things that had happened while he was gone and warned him of the CURSE. The Witch Doctor had confessed about the EVIL plans he and Dragonfly had made.

But Chief Tyanne absolutely refused to tell him where Melody was. "I am sorry Harlan, things are looking very bad and there is nothing you can do about it!" The Chief sternly warned him. "It is best for all of us if you go back to your own people and never come here again!" Harlan would not listen to these words; he knew he: MUST find her!

So Harlan began his search. He asked everyone he met and then rode many miles to other Indian tribes to find her but no luck. Where could she be? Dragonfly began to follow him here and there, trying to stop him from finding his sister. They had many bitter and threatening words and soon it was an all-out battle with angry fists flying both of them were hurt but Dragonfly was the most seriously injured. He rode off into the mountains to be alone and try to recover. Harlan rode on, even though hurt; he was determined to find Melody!

CHAPTER FOUR

There is a change of scene here;

Dusty is speaking; *"Oh Silky what are we going to do, Melody really needs us but my foot is still so sore and my wing has a torn spot. I can barely fly?"*

"We must return to Master Tory Toad!", said Silky. "But he will be so angry because we have disobeyed the Code of Harmony, rules," replied Dusty.

"I am sure he already knows what has happened. All the animals and birds report everything we do to him, so let's face the music and make the trip up to Castle Rock. It may take days to find him but I know he will help us," she replied.

"But I am scared of what he will say and anyway I not sure I can make the trip."

"We can get help if we have too. Rudy Hummingbird flies like no other bird and he is always ready and willing to help a friend. I will find him and ask him to go with us.", Silky replied, as she gracefully stretched out her long shiny wings and soared away.

When Rudy Hummingbird heard the story of Harlan and Melody, he agreed to help his friends Dusty and Silky. First he preened his feathers and then got an extra big drink of flower nectar and he was ready to go. It was several days with many long hard miles of flying. Up along the splashing waters of the bigger of the two creeks they went until they reached the rugged rock canyon. They were a strange looking trio, flying mostly by night. When Dusty got too tired Rudy gently pulled him along by his long foretop and soon they were right above Castle Rock. But where was Master Tory Toad? A helpful Blue Jay called to them and led the way on up towards the special caves above the rocky ledges. By now even Rudy was quite tired. They thanked him for all the help and he was off for home.

Now they must face Master Tory Toad himself!

They walked slowly into the darkest back part of his abode and heard a low gruff voice say, *"You may enter and present your case."* Dusty wanted to fly back out but Silky held onto his tail. We can do this she kept whispering into his ear. After they blurted out the whole story of Melody and Harlan (conveniently leaving out where they had helped things along), Master Tory Toad gave them a stern lecture reminding the two of them about the Code of Harmony Rules, do not interfere in the ways of humans when there is bad trouble and wars. After a quiet, restful night in the cave they meet him again in the morning and he magically mended Dusty torn wing and gave him a special medicine from the beautiful ferns growing in the cave. The next morning Dusty's leg was well and strong again. Still speaking in his natural gravelly voice, Master Tory Toad! warned them about breaking the rules but because it was done in a sincere attempt to help people he gave them his blessings. He explained to them, they must use their HEAD as well as their HEART, if they were going to help fix this problem! He said, there was a lot of work yet to be done. But things would work out all right with a special surprise ending if they did their job well. They thanked him and feeling encouraged and refreshed left for the trip back to Forest Ranch.

Rudy Hummingbird helps Dusty

CHAPTER FIVE
....

Meanwhile Harlan continued his search. He rode east, then west, and then south but he hadn't gone north, and that is where Melody was! The Animal Chat Line was working and the Harmonies KNEW where she was. How to tell Harlan? How to get him moving in the right direction? Dusty and Silky flew on up ahead of him and using all their might, put large rocks in the trail but he easily just moved them aside and rode on.

It was almost springtime and the Dogwood flowers were staring to bloom. Would he find her this time? What to do? Master Tory Toad had said, you must be smart and do things right, but how?

"Wait a minute I know what we can do! Let's lay a trail the right way (heading north) We can pick branches of Dogwood flowers and shape them like arrows pointing the right way at every turn.", said Silky.

"Oh Silky, that is a lot of work. What if late tonight we just whispered into Stick's ear GO NORTH?"

"Well we might get poor Stick into trouble if we got him to disobey his master."

"O.K. you are right let's go with the flowers, maybe Harlan will get the idea."

So they labored all night laying beautiful white flowering branches in arrow shaped patterns at every turn in the trail. The next day when Harlan came to the branches of flowers he was very puzzled. He knew something strange was going on? But he and Stick were also getting very tired and so they stopped for a drink and to rest a bit. Now horses like to eat many things and some flowers, like Dogwood blooms taste delicious to them. So when Harlan wasn't looking, Stick got his reins untied and managed to wander up the path eating his way all along. When Harlan finally found him they were so far into the northern trail, that he decided to keep going that direction. Yeahhhh he was getting closer!

Then he found her! At first she refused to talk to him or even look at him, but broken hearts can be mended. So later after much persuasion he convinced her of his reasons for not returning sooner, he also told her of the fight he had with her brother and all about the EVIL CURSE. Together they must find a way to overcome this awful CURSE! When she saw the Gold Nugget that he wore around his neck, she tearfully told him how she had lost the matching crystal necklace, and that it was still in the bottom of the Pool.

CHAPTER SIX

They were so thankful to be back together but: *"Not so fast cowboy!"* The Indian tribe she was staying with was not willing to let Melody leave with this stranger. They did not trust him and she had been very ill. Harlan convinced them of his good intentions by helping them battle a marauding band of an enemy tribe. He also made many friends among them and went on several hunting trips for a good supply of deer meat. It was a happy spring because this time Harlan was there with Melody when the White flowers bloomed! It was nearing summer when they finally returned together to her home in the meadow.

Chief Tyanne, her friends and loved ones were all very happy to see her and they noticed how well she looked. The color had returned to her cheeks and Harlan had returned with her that was the best part.

Meanwhile, up in the high country Dragonfly was recovering from his injuries. One night he had a dream and in the dream the – Life Spirit of the Mountains spoke to him. *"You are selfish and wrong to wish harm on these people, you must change your ways and then you can be accepted and forgiven for the evil things you have done!"* Down deep inside he really cared about his sister Melody and felt very sorry for the problems he had caused her. He decided when he was able to travel he would return and find them and warn everyone about the EVIL Curse. He knew that the CURSE was much more than having Harlan to forget his plans, because if anyone even disturbed the water trying to get more gold nuggets out of the Pool, it was rigged to the large rocks on top of the mountains and they might be killed!

Several days later, Harlan and Melody and all who wanted to help went to the Pool and tried to recover the gold and the necklace, not knowing the full danger. But sadly poor mixed-up Dragonfly himself was the one killed when he rushed to **WARN** them. Suddenly the earth shook with a landslide and many huge boulders fell into the Pool all because of the CURSE but no one else was hurt: just poor Dragonfly. In the vain attempt to rescue him, Harlan lost the leather bag with the white horses on the front and all the gold nuggets with it.

Late that night as they were grieving for Dragonfly, there was a big storm with terrible hail, thunder and lightning upon the mountains. Early the next morning Harlan went alone to the Pool and tried to retrieve the gold nuggets and look for Dragonfly but because of the landslide it was all gone, perhaps forever. It was all deep under the water covered by the rocks. The only thing he recovered was Melody's crystal necklace.

While Harlan was standing there looking into the dark water he suddenly felt different, light headed with a clear mind, and then he realized the CURSE WAS BROKEN! Everyone around the country heard the story and they were warned to NEVER search for gold in or even near the Heart-Shaped Pool!

But something else had happened that same night as the storm subsided, haunting music could be heard high upon the mountains. When the lightning stopped and the sky cleared, a strange looking ray of light fell from the full moon and it hit the Pool. Even though no one was there to see it, SOMETHING MAGIC HAPPENED! In the misty bubbling water, strange white crystal balls were formed. Then deep near the piles of rock and sand these strange glassy balls slowly changed into crystal ponies! In the warmth of the morning sunlight the baby HARMONIES were hatched!

These tiny creatures had the wings of a dragonfly plus a long white fuzzy mane and tail, when it dried out. Where their feet touched the ground little golden hoof prints were left behind and soon as their wings uncurled they could fly!

That is the Harmony Legend of Forest Ranch.

From that day to this people tell of seeing the delightfully beautiful ponies and they call them Harmonies. Near the Pool in Big Chico Creek is a warning carved into the rocks high on the canyon wall. Note: it is dangerous to climb up there! But it reads: -TAKE GOLD FROM THIS POOL AND EVIL FOREVER YOUR HEART WILL RULE- The breeze makes a lonesome sound when it passes over the headstone left there in memory of Dragonfly.

The story goes on but not much. Melody fashioned the quartz crystal necklace into part of her white deerskin wedding dress and she and Harlan were married right next to the Heart-Shaped Pool. It was the largest celebration the town of Forest Ranch had ever had. For the first time in history of the country there was singing, dancing, and feasting, with all of the loggers, miners, plus people from town and the Indian tribes from all directions coming to attend the wedding. Wise old Chief Tyanne gave away the bride. With so many people working together the gold was not needed. Rumor has it that Harlan and Melody had several children and lived many happy years in a little cabin near the Forks of the Butte.

The Wedding at the Pool

Near Butte Meadows

After the gold rush was over, it was rumored that Harlan became a logger.

What happened to Dusty and Silky? Well Master Tory Toad, was so pleased with the work they did, he put them in charge of teaching and training all the newly hatched young Harmonies. Note: they still took time to visit with and check on Melody.

My yarn is winding down but even today many people claim to hear the hauntingly beautiful melodies coming from the many streams and waterfalls in Northern California. Some folks claim to have seen the crystal ponies with wings. I have never seen one of them but on occasion I am still out there searching. I can imagine how they might look (see my pictures). I may still be a bit too young? Please note: they are usually seen in early morning or late evening and mostly by the very young or much older folks. If you take the name of Harlan and Melody and mix it together a bit, you come close to the name of Harmony. Oh, I bet you noticed that already didn't you?

Would you like to have a peek? at one? The best advice I can give you is to go to a mountain stream and sit very still and listen. If you hear pleasant sounds, then look very carefully near the water. Note: it must be clean running water with NO litter about!

So please remember to carry a bag and carefully clean up the area first. Harmonies hate litter and trash, so you MUST pick it up. They are usually seen in pairs and often in snow or ice and always around the water. Even though they leave specks of gold in their tiny hoof prints don't go for the gold it is just too hard to scrape up.

The old gentleman with the long white whiskers is in the local Forest Ranch cemetery. The World's Largest Cherry Tree fell down. My kids grew up and had kids and their kids had kids too. But the Diamond Match Co., water trough is still right there. Thanks for letting me spin my YARN but it took quite a while and I still have work to do.

Note: Harmonies cause lighthearted feelings and clear thinking so even if you don't see them it doesn't mean a thing because they may still be RIGHT there. Also you might take a little time to enjoy the scenery. If you DO see one, I suggest you keep it a SECRET or only tell ME.

Please remember that Ireland has a Blarney Stone and Scotland has the Loch Ness Monster, so why can't Forest Ranch, California have a little Harmony?

P.S. You might try the fishing too!

Wilma R. Forester

3½ in. at the shoulder
crystal clear, transparent wings
white mane and tail

HARMONEY
(HARMONESE)

Rudy Hummingbird helps Dusty

Chasing a Butterfly

The End

ABOUT THE AUTHOR AND THE ARTIST—
WILMA RAE ANDERSON, ROLLS, FORESTER

"Wilma you are going to get an A on the story you wrote in your High School English Class." said my teacher. Wow I didn't get many A's so I was surprised and pleased. "Maybe someday you will become a writer," she continued. I didn't think so I was too much into riding and training my horse and chasing boys.

I was born in Los Angeles, California in 1933 and we had NO books at home to read. Most books were very expensive and our family just could not afford any thing like that. Then one day my father bought a new set of encyclopedias' called *The Book of Knowledge*. There were at least ten books and even at five years old I loved every one of them. I would spend hours going through the pages and studying the pictures and enjoying the Aesop Fables. We, (the Anderson family, mom dad and three kids plus our dog Boogie) move to Chico, California in 1940 or so. We lived in several different places and finally settled in the barren wastelands of a part of town called Pleasant Valley. Ours was the only house on the left side of Cactus Avenue. My older brother and sister (Clinton, and Barbara,) and I walked the two miles to the one room school Pleasant Valley on East Avenue. It was great horse country and easy access to Bidwell Park. I am still writing stories about my many adventures in the Park.

I married young and had two sons and a daughter, James Steven, (deceased) Gene Jeffery and Brenda Jean. Our family moved to forest Ranch, California in 1964. My name is now Wilma Rae Forester. I have trophies and ribbons from riding a painting but being a Christian: **To you O Lord, I lift up my soul: in you I trust, O my God. Psalms. 25:1-2**, and my children, grandchildren and great grand children are the things I boast about the most.

I am an artist first but I love to write, whether it is Fiction or Nonfiction. Of course I get to illustrate all of my stories. Sometimes when I am deep into telling a tale it feels like I have stepped into another world and it is a wonderful world of privacy and freedom where I alone am in control. I truly enjoy writing and painting.

Wilma Rae Forester

10620 Treena Street, Suite 230
San Diego, California,
CA 92131 USA
www.readersmagnet.com
1.619.354.2643
Copyright 2022 All Rights Reserved

www.ingramcontent.com/pod-product-compliance
Lightning Source LLC
LaVergne TN
LVHW070436080526
838202LV00034B/2651